D0872519

Vacation Time

Vacation Time

Poems for Children
by Nikki Giovanni

Illustrated by Marisabina Russo

William Morrow and Company, Inc.
New York   1980

Library of Congress Cataloging in Publication Data

Giovanni, Nikki.
   Vacation time.

   SUMMARY: Includes 22 poems on a variety of topics.
1. Children's poetry, American. [1. American
poetry] I. Title.
PS3557.I55V3   811'.54   79-91643
ISBN 0-688-03657-0

Printed in the United States of America

First Edition
1 2 3 4 5 6 7 8 9 10

Book Design by Michael Mauceri

Vacation Time is dedicated to
the third-grade class at Bush School
and especially my friend Stephen

Contents

Vacation Time

Vacation Time

What should I write
    a poem about
I asked my eight year old son
"Something good" he said to me
"Something that would be fun"

I tried to think
    what fun could mean
    to me feeling old and wry
All the bills paid and a broken spade
    in the middle of July
"All the bills paid and a broken spade
    in the middle of July!"
Incredulously he looked at me
"Please tell me the reason why"

The reason why is the reason
    because when I'm feeling old
    and wry
    with all the bills paid
    and a *broken* spade
Vacation time is nigh

Snowflakes

Little   boys   are   like
    Snowflakes
No   two   are   alike

Missing   teeth   skinned   elbows
    Always
Stinky   sticky   slippery
    Sweaty   and   Sweet

Jonathan Sitting in Mud

Michael is meaner
than Hal who is keener
than Jonathan sitting in mud

Ida the cow
lets out a big "Wow!"
when she starts to chewing her cud

There's a brass ring
on the Merry Go Thing
but it got drowned in the flood

His Father said "Hey!
Won't you come in today?"
But Jonathan stayed in the mud

Jonathan sat in the mud
all day
Jonathan sat in the mud
His Mother cried
His Father tried
But Jonathan sat in the mud

It's been a week
without a peak
from Jonathan sitting in mud

Lurleen the spider
keeps getting wider
as she sits on the rose bud

And Jonathan said
as he stretched out for bed
"I'm happy where I am"

And so as we leave him
though others may grieve him
Jonathan stays on the lam

Jonathan sat in the mud
all day
Jonathan sat in the mud
His Mother cried
His Father tried
But Jonathan sat in the mud

Strawberry Patches

Through the green clover   and white-tipped violets
and brown-flecked bunnies   and laughing pin-striped
                                  chipmunks

            (Being very careful
        of the dandelions shedding
         their yellow spring coats)

Little girls   tip toe   into the meadows
                        playing hide
                          and seek

            in the strawberry patch

Paula the Cat

Paula the cat
not thin nor fat
is as happy as house cats can be

She reads and she writes
with all the delights
of intelligent cats up a tree

Tired of the view
she chose to pursue
a fate unbeknownst to the crowd

Finding a boat
locked up in a moat
she boarded and shouted out loud

I'm Paula the cat
not thin nor fat
as happy as house cats can be

But now I've the urge
for my spirit to surge
and I shall go off
to sea

Yolandé the Panda

Yolandé the panda
sat with Amanda
eating a bar-be-cue rib

They drank a beer
and gave a big cheer
"Hooray! for women's lib"

Prickled Pickles Don't Smile

Never tickle
a prickled pickle
cause prickled pickles
Don't smile

Never goad
a loaded toad
when he has to walk
A whole mile

Froggies go courting
with weather reporting
that indicates
There are no snows

But always remember
the month of December
is very hard
On your nose

The Dragonfly

A dragonfly sat
    on my nose
I wish it had sat
    on my toes
I guess nobody
    ever knows
Where a dragonfly will sit

Kisses

Flowers for hours
    remain inert
but when the bees pass
    they flutter and flirt

The bees come down
    to steal a kiss
then off they fly
    to some other miss

Houses

Little kangaroos   i think
prefer to live in pouches

Little boys and little girls
prefer to live in houses
Sometimes

Eskimos live in igloos
Indians in a tent

But you and i live in a rat hole
where we pay no rent

Jessica, a Bird Who Sings

Jessica's a bird who sings
even though she's clipped her wings
Just so she could feather up
her nest

Mother birds do always try
even though they sometimes cry
Wishing they could get
a little rest

Jessie knows when day is through
she did what she had to do
'Cause she'd never give her love
in jest

All the birdies in her tree
sing to her with hearts of glee
Mother bird we think
You are the best

The Lady in the Chair

Little Bru and little Chris
Every morning give a kiss
To the lady sitting in the chair

In her rocker she does stay
Neat and prim throughout the day
Gold and silver sprinkled in her hair

She is old and she has known
All the ways the wind has blown
Now she watches life without a care

In the evening before bed
Just before the prayers are said
Grandma Lou gets out her chocolate treat

Three small pieces she does break
Two to give and one to take
Sharing with her greatgrandsons a sweet

Little Bru and little Chris
Every evening give a kiss
To the lady sitting in the chair

I Only Watch the Bubbles

Mommy watches the soap
when I wash dishes

Gram watches the soaps
most afternoons

Dad looks for the soap
that is on sale

I only watch the bubbles
when I bathe

I only watch the bubbles
when I bathe

They turn into so many
different things

I spread them out on me
I can be anything

I only watch the bubbles
when I bathe

The Sun

Sunsets are so pretty
the clouds and colors leap
Across her deep red belly
as she flutters off to sleep

I also like the sunrise
I really like to feel
The sunbeams walk across me
from my head to my heel

Rainbows

If I could climb
    the mountains
And rest on clouds
    that float
I'd swim across
    the clear blue air
To reach my rainbow boat

My rainbow boat
    is oh so big
And I could be
    so tall
As I sit
    in my captain's chair
The master of it all

But I am just a little boy
    who's standing on the ground
And others steer
    the rainbow past
While I just hang around

I sit on the ground
    and see
The rainbows steering
    right past me
I sit on the ground
And wonder *why*

The Stars

Across the dark and quiet sky
When sunbeams have to go to bed
The stars peep out and sparkle up
    Occasionally they fall

They dance the ballet of the night
They pirouette and boogie down
In blue and red and blue-white dress
    They hustle through the night

The fairies play among the stars
They ride on carpets of gold dust
And Dawn's gray fingers shake them off
    Occasionally they fall

The Reason I Like Chocolate

The reason I like chocolate
is I can lick my fingers
and nobody tells me I'm not polite

I especially like scary movies
'cause I can snuggle with Mommy
or my big sister and they don't laugh

I like to cry sometimes 'cause
everybody says "what's the matter
don't cry"

and I like books
for all those reasons
but mostly 'cause they just make me
happy

and I really like
to be happy

Tommy's Mommy

Mommy did you bring my flippers
Tommy asked his Mommy

Is that all you have to say
Mommy asked her Tommy

Did you bring my diving mask
Tommy asked his Mommy

Is that all you have to say
Mommy asked her Tommy

Did you bring my snorkel
Tommy asked his Mommy

Is that all you have to say
Mommy asked her Tommy

I love you Mommy
Tommy said Did you bring them Did you

I love you Tommy Mommy said
Yes I brought them to you

Masks

Sis wears a mask
when she makes a scene

Dad wears a mask
when he is mean

I wear my mask
when it's Halloween

But Mom wears her mask
for beauty purposes

Joy

In school today
we studied joy

"I had joy once"
I volunteered

"When everybody thought
we were going to lose
I hit a home run"

"How did it feel"
the teacher asked
I said "I had joy"

And he said "No, you don't
have joy
You feel it"

I am very confused
I was very joyful
'til he said I wasn't

Teachers are funny
I think

Covers

Glass covers windows
    to keep the cold away
Clouds cover the sky
    to make a rainy day

Nighttime covers
    all the things that creep
Blankets cover me
    when I'm asleep

Good Night

Goodnight Mommy
Goodnight Dad

I kiss them as I go

Goodnight Teddy
Goodnight Spot

The moonbeams call me so

I climb the stairs
Go down the hall
And walk into my room

My day of play is ending
But my night of sleep's in bloom